Travels of Bumpzee and Swendee

The Cloudy Twins Meet Toughball —

A Children's Book About the Outdoors, Nature, Kindness and Friendship

Printed in the United States of America

Library of Congress Control Number: 2021911819

ISBN: 978-1-7373252-0-8

Dedication

This book is dedicated to all my grandchildren (including those still to come).

Travels of Bumpzee and Swendee was inspired during a road trip from Maskwacis in Alberta, Canada, through the Rocky Mountains of British Columbia, with my Cree Nation daughter-in-law.

Acknowledgment

Special gratitude and thanks to my husband, Gary, who has never wavered in his encouragement and support of this book.

Once upon a time, on the snowcapped mountains of British Columbia —

No! No! Twice upon a time lived baby twin clouds named Bumpzee and Swendee. The only way the other clouds could tell them apart was by the bumps on Bumpzee's tail end.

They were twin clouds who did everything together. Bumpzee and his sister Swendee were happy clouds who had yet to start their journey across the mountains to reach the kingdom of the Big Tail Cloud Tribe, which is where all the other Big Tail Clouds lived with their families.

One bright, early spring day in May, the twins heard a big yawn coming from the other side of the mountain. Bumpzee and Swendee quickly floated over to the other side to see where the noise came from. To their surprise, they saw a baby snowball sitting on a rock on the side of the mountain.

"What's your name?" asked Bumpzee. The snowball opened his eyes as wide as wide can be. He thought that only Mountain Snow People talked, and he had never talked to clouds before. The snowball answered in a sad, soft voice, "My name is Toughball."

Swendee then asked Toughball why he looked so sad. Toughball said he felt sad because he could not join his sisters and brothers at the bottom of the mountain. He had missed the first rainfall, and rain was necessary for him to begin his journey down the mountain.

"Why didn't you go with your family when they left?" the twins asked Toughball.

"You see," Toughball said, "I consider myself an explorer, as my grandfather was. While exploring the caves with my friends, I lost track of time."

Toughball then begged the twin clouds to help him join his family and all the fun at the bottom of the mountains.

The twins thought and thought and thought and thought about how they could help Toughball reach the bottom of the mountains.

Bumpzee said, "Let's roll him down the mountain like a cannonball."

Toughball replied, "No, no, that won't work. I'd break apart. I need to melt first."

Swendee then suggested that they call the other clouds for help. So, they called and they called, but the other clouds were so far away that they couldn't hear them.

Swendee and Bumpzee couldn't figure out a way to help their new friend Toughball. Feeling sad and helpless, they began to cry. Their bodies began to change color from white to gray.

Just then, to Toughball's surprise, he noticed that the top of his head had started to melt! When they realized what was happening, Bumpzee and Swendee began puffing their cheeks as much as they could to blow more rain into the air.

Quickly, before Toughball's mouth disappeared along with his voice, he thanked his new friends Bumpzee and Swendee for their help. Then he rolled over to the crack at the side of the mountain to begin his long journey to the bottom of the mountains.

25

Bumpzee and Swendee looked down with much excitement and joy as Toughball made his way to join his family. As he melted down the mountain, they could hear his laughter.

With big smiles on their faces, Bumpzee and Swendee continued their journey home to the kingdom of the Big Tail Cloud Tribe.

Interesting and Fun Facts About the Natural Habitat of the Cloudy Twins:

1.   The First Nation people call the region "Big Sky Country." "First Nation" is a term used to describe the indigenous peoples, who are the original inhabitants of the land now called Canada.

2.   British Colombia (BC) is the westernmost province of Canada, situated between the Pacific Ocean and the Rocky Mountains.

3.   Snow-capped is a term used mainly in the warmer months, when the snow has melted on most of the mountains but remains on the top, appearing as though the mountains are wearing caps.

4.   The reindeer here are called caribou by the First Nation peoples. The woodland caribou are considered the largest bodied reindeer, with bulls weighing more than 400 pounds. Caribou, as part of the deer family, have large hooves and long legs to support their bulk in the snow.

5.   Elk are the largest and heaviest species in the deer family. An elk's antlers, which only grow on bulls, are fast-growing bones, which can grow as much as one inch in a day. They look so cool!

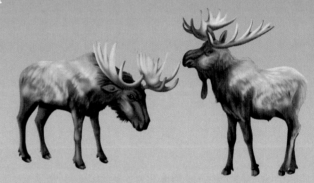

6.   Mountain goats, also known as Rocky Mountain goats, are hoofed mammals that can jump as much as twelve feet in one leap. Their coats are double layers that shed in the summer and provide warmth in the winter.

7. Bighorn sheep are known for their large horns. A pair of horns can weigh as much as 14 kilograms (30 pounds). They are able to survive extreme heat in the summer and cold in the winter. They escape the heat by resting in the shade of the trees and caves during the day. They can live up to 15 years. Male bighorns compete in head-to-head combat.

8. Ravens are extremely smart. They can imitate human speech and communicate using their beaks and wings like hand gestures. They can fly upside down and do somersaults in flight, and they love to play.

9. Rocky Mountain black bears, even with their bulky size, are good at climbing trees. They are three feet tall when standing on all four feet. They rarely turn down a snack. Black bears love to eat a variety of summer berries.

10. The water cycle is evident in the Rocky Mountains and valleys of British Columbia. This is the cycle in which rain and snow run off the mountains to collect in lakes and rivers below. When the sun heats the lakes and rivers, the water comes back into the air and clouds form. When the clouds become heavy with water, they release rain or snow, and the cycle begins again!

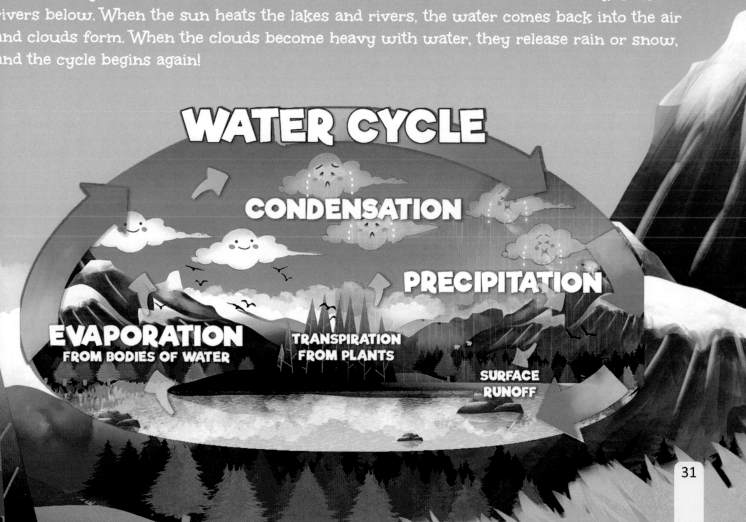

WATER CYCLE

CONDENSATION

PRECIPITATION

EVAPORATION
FROM BODIES OF WATER

TRANSPIRATION
FROM PLANTS

SURFACE
RUNOFF